Georgie and
the Planet Raider

Julia Jarman
and Damon Burnard

Collin

There are lots of Jets to read and enjoy

Georgie and the Dragon
by Julia Jarman and Damon Burnard

Monty the Dog Who Wears Glasses,
Monty Bites Back, Monty Must be Magic
by Colin West

Mossop's Last Chance, Jigger's Day Off,
Martians at Mudpuddle Farm
by Michael Morpurgo and Shoo Rayner

First published in Great Britain by
A & C Black (Publishers) Ltd. in 1993.
First published by Young Lions in 1993
and reprinted by Collins in 1995.

Collins is an imprint of HarperCollins*Publishers* Ltd,
77-85 Fulham Palace Road,
Hammersmith, London W6 8JB.

ISBN 978-0-00-674495-5

Chapter One

Georgie Bell, computer ace, was resting. When she last played on her computer something weird had happened. She had nearly been eaten by a dragon, yes really! Her brilliant brain had saved her, just, but she didn't want to risk that again.

'You can't play with my computer,' said Georgie.

The Tank was Georgie's little sister.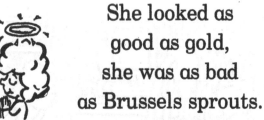
She looked as
good as gold,
she was as bad
as Brussels sprouts.
But she had helped when Georgie
was in trouble, and Georgie was
supposed to be looking after her.

'No, Tank! It's dangerous.' Georgie
had unplugged the computer, but
she still didn't trust it.

Tank
want!

Tank can't have.
Come here and
play tiddly-winks!

She was kicking the tiddly-winks
angrily across the room when the
doorbell rang.

Georgie went to answer it.
She realised almost immediately
(well half-way down the stairs) that
leaving the Tank alone was a mistake,
but by the time she got
back it was too late.

Chapter Two

The Tank had plugged
in the computer . . .

. . . rammed in a disc . . .

. . . and pounded the keys.

'Stop!' yelled Georgie, but it was too late. The Tank was already hurtling through the screen!

Georgie pounded
the RETURN key.
She pounded the EXIT key.
She held it down. She prayed.

And the spinning screen went into
reverse! There was a

But out of the smoke stepped,

a DRAGON!

Chapter Three

It was the one who had nearly
eaten her.

'What have you done with the Tank?'
cried Georgie.
'I think I passed her on the way in,'
said the dragon. Clearly he wasn't
bothered. Georgie was.

'Oh, I wouldn't worry about that,
Georgie dear,' said the dragon.
He was licking his lips.
'Why not?' said Georgie.

And with that he grabbed her. He told Georgie that although she'd tricked him once, it would never happen again. He was going to eat her now, *raw*. Georgie thought fast.

It was a good ruse. The dragon had three children of whom he was immensely proud. He loved talking about them.

'Yes,' sighed the dragon (Georgie began to cheer up – she had seen something on the screen which gave her hope). 'Deidre is such a clever girl. She already knows what a damsel is and what a damsel is for' . . . and that reminded him.

'You're a damsel, Georgie.' He flexed his jaws.

'Yes, but Dragon,' said Georgie, 'can you see what I see?' She pointed to the screen.

The dragon was trembling. He started to paw at the screen to absolutely no effect.

He must get home, he said, to Daphne, Dennis and Deidre. He should never have left them all alone. 'No,' said Georgie, 'you shouldn't.'

A monster was
knocking at the door
of the dragon's lair.

'Don't open it!'
the dragon cried,
but it was no use.

14

Chapter Four

'Georgie?' The dragon's voice was small and pleading.

'What, Dragon?'

'You're very clever. Can't you d-do something?'

Georgie pressed STOP, but it didn't work. The monster didn't stop. He was galloping towards a spaceship. Then Georgie saw something which made the situation even more desperate.

There was the Tank! She was in the
monster's net, trying to bite her
way out!
And the monster was singing,
'Fee, fi, fo, foo,
You are going in my zoo!'
as he stuffed her into the back of
the spaceship with the three young
dragons.

Georgie realised what must have happened.

Chapter Five

PLANET RAIDER was her hardest game. She had beaten the monster only once! And he had never forgiven her!

His horrible face leered from the screen.

'Ha! You'll be for it now, Georgie!'

Wait until your mum gets back!

'Do something, Georgie!' The dragon was desperate. So was Georgie. Drawing on her vast knowledge of computer games she pressed STOP.

She pressed PAUSE.

She pressed
VERTICAL HOLD
very hard,
hoping the vibrations
would shake the prisoners out of
the spaceship. That had worked in
the past. It didn't work now.
Nothing did. Georgie felt powerless.
The monster was out-thinking her,
and he knew it.

The dragon stared defiantly at the monster.

'You!' The monster sneered. 'You!' He spat scornfully.

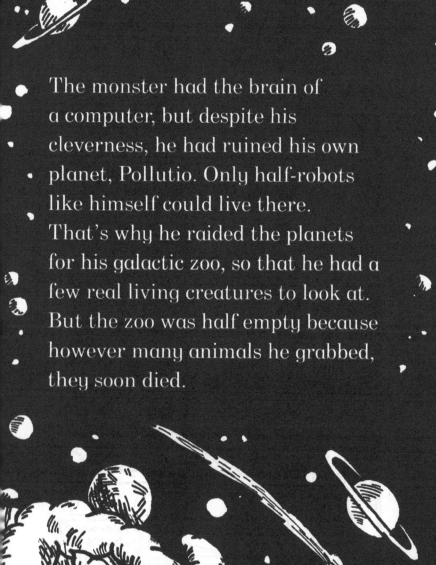

The monster had the brain of
a computer, but despite his
cleverness, he had ruined his own
planet, Pollutio. Only half-robots
like himself could live there.
That's why he raided the planets
for his galactic zoo, so that he had a
few real living creatures to look at.
But the zoo was half empty because
however many animals he grabbed,
they soon died.

And now Planet Raider was returning to Pollutio, despite Georgie's efforts to stop him. There was a deafening roar as his spaceship zoomed away.

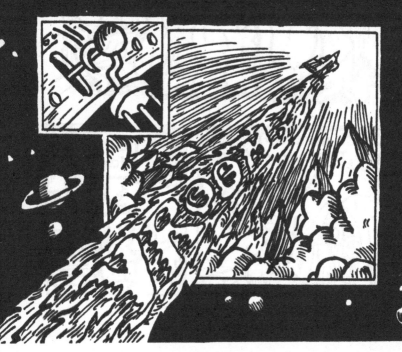

Tears sizzled down the dragon's nostrils. Wounded by the insult to his intelligence, miserable at the loss of his children, he crawled under Georgie's bedclothes.

If only she could make it work.
Quickly she pounded the keyboard
of her computer and scanned the
menu which came up.

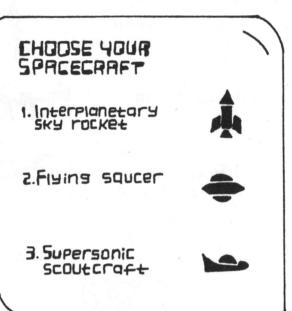

CHOOSE YOUR
SPACECRAFT

1. Interplanetary
   sky rocket

2. Flying saucer

3. Supersonic
   scoutcraft

Hmmm..

Georgie chose the
supersonic scoutcraft.

Another menu came up.

CHOOSE YOUR WEAPON

1. Double-edged
   cybernetic sword

2. Lazer gun

3. Robotic
   master key

Georgie chose the robotic master key.
It looked a bit like a tin-opener.
The dragon peeped out from under
the bedclothes, 'What are you
doing, Georgie?'

She tossed him the computer manual.

Then she bashed ENTER and
SPACE. Nothing happened.

Still nothing happened.
Then her computer began to hum,
and . . .

Chapter Six

VROOSH!

First she shrank,
then she hurtled
through the screen.

Seconds later she was flying straight into space in her supersonic scoutcraft . . .

. . . just as Georgie's mum came home.

Chapter Seven

But Georgie wasn't there of course.
She was searching space for Planet
Raider.

Close on his tail, she whizzed past Mars, dodging flying asteroids.

Then she passed Jupiter, just avoiding the Great Red Spot, a whirling storm that had been raging for over 300 years.

She passed Saturn,

Uranus

and Neptune.

But only when she had passed all nine planets of the Solar System and was passing Mars for the second time, did she realise that she had been going round in a circle.

She had been on a
galactic wild goose chase!

I've been tricked!

Did Georgie give up? No. She used her brilliant brain to continue her rescue mission.

Georgie changed direction and headed for the unknown!

Meanwhile, back in Georgie's bedroom, the dragon was using his brilliant brain . . .

. . . and with the help of his computer expertise . . .

. . . Georgie shot forward into OVERDRIVE.

There was Planet Raider, approaching Pollutio.

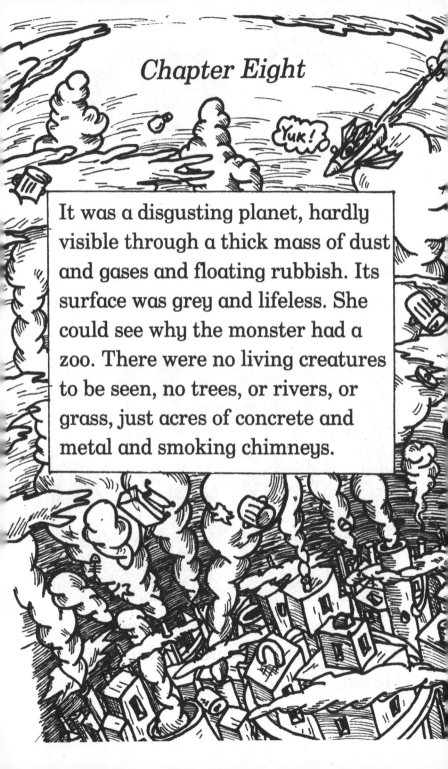

Chapter Eight

Yuk!

It was a disgusting planet, hardly visible through a thick mass of dust and gases and floating rubbish. Its surface was grey and lifeless. She could see why the monster had a zoo. There were no living creatures to be seen, no trees, or rivers, or grass, just acres of concrete and metal and smoking chimneys.

Georgie landed the scoutcraft
behind a pile of rubbish. She could
hear Planet Raider instructing the
robot-drones to put his latest
specimens into the zoo.

'I'll be round to see them later,'
he said. Right now he was hungry.
He was off to re-energise.

Georgie got out of the scoutcraft.

Fortunately, the zoo was clearly sign-posted.

Unfortunately, Georgie was very conspicuous.

Pollutions were huge and grey and metallic. She was small and pink and squidgy.

But by dodging behind heaps of rubbish she managed to follow the crowds, until . . .

. . . a Pollution child saw her.

Georgie froze – and the child picked her up.

And luckily for Georgie,
Tinnitus got her way, and
Georgie got hers.
Into the zoo they went.

Chapter Nine

There was the Tank in a cage labelled 'Latest Acquisitions'. In fact, the Tank and the dragons and a sick-looking kangaroo were the only acquisitions. All the others must have died.

Georgie had to admire the Tank's spirit. She was still trying to bite her way out, and she was urging her companions to do the same. The trouble was, they just weren't strong enough.

But help was at hand! For back home in Georgie's bedroom, the dragon had picked up the manual again, and had just come across a word he recognised.

Eager to prove he had a brain, he spelled the word out on the keyboard –

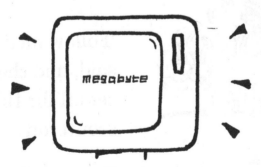

It had an amazing effect.

Terrified, the Pollutions ran off.

Georgie hurried over to the Tank.

'Follow me,' she said, and they all set off for the scoutcraft.

But the scoutcraft wasn't there.
In its place stood Planet Raider.
With a horrible snarl he scooped
them up in his net.

'You'll never escape,' he sneered.

Chapter Ten

Still Georgie didn't give up.
'Blow, dragons!' she ordered, and
Dennis, Daphne and Deidre puffed
furiously . . .

. . . and behind the smoke screen,
Georgie and the Tank took
megabytes out of the net.

Then there was a desperate fight. Georgie, the Tank and the dragons took megabytes out of Planet Raider.

He fought back, punching and kicking.

Georgie and Co. didn't give in.

Nor did Planet Raider.

Then he made a big mistake . . .

. . . and was out for the count.

Chapter Eleven

Georgie opened him up with the robotic master key and changed his computer programme from Planet Raider to Planet Aider.

'I don't get it,' said the Tank.
Georgie explained that now the
monster would stop raiding and
start aiding the planet, helping to
clean it up for a start.
The transformation had already
begun.

And he was!

'And us,' said the Tank, 'Georgie and me, we want to go home too.' The question was how?

Some say (the dragon for instance) that what happened next was a stroke of genius. Others say it was an Amazing Coincidence, but it was certainly a fact that seconds after the Tank spoke, the dragon, playing one of his very own computer games . . .

. . . hit the EXIT key and suddenly . . .

Chapter Twelve

. . . they were all flying, through time and space and the computer screen into Georgie's bedroom.

But the dragon
was already
thinking
of recipes.

Pointing to Georgie and the Tank
he said,

Georgie was shocked.

But the dragon
was heading for
the kitchen . . .

. . . just as Georgie's
mum was coming
up the stairs.

He had never seen anything as
fierce as Georgie's mum.

As the dragon backed into the bedroom, Georgie slipped DRAGONS GO HOME into the disc drive.

I think you'd better be off!

Then she pressed RETURN and the screen started to suck and spin.

Then, where moments before there had been four dragons, there were now four puffs of smoke.